Pippin's Big Jump

First published in 2002 by
Franklin Watts
96 Leonard Street
London
EC2A 4XD

Franklin Watts Australia
56 O'Riordan Street
Alexandria
NSW 2015

A CIP catalogue record for this book is available
from the British Library.

ISBN 0 7496 4703 5 (hbk)
ISBN 0 7496 4710 8 (pbk)

Series Editor: Jackie Hamley
Series Advisor: Dr Barrie Wade
Cover Design: Jason Anscomb
Design: Peter Scoulding

Printed in Hong Kong

For Olivia Solomon – HR

Pippin's
Big Jump

by Hilary Robinson and Sarah Warburton

W
FRANKLIN WATTS
LONDON•SYDNEY

Some penguins are
afraid of the dark.

Some penguins are afraid
of creaking icebergs.

But this penguin, Pippin, was
afraid of jumping into the sea!

"Come on Pippin," said Ma
Penguin, gently. "Watch
the other penguins."

Pippin watched nervously as they
jumped off the iceberg and played
in the cool, blue sea.

"Why don't you have a go, Pippin?" Ma suggested. Pippin stood quietly, shaking with fear.

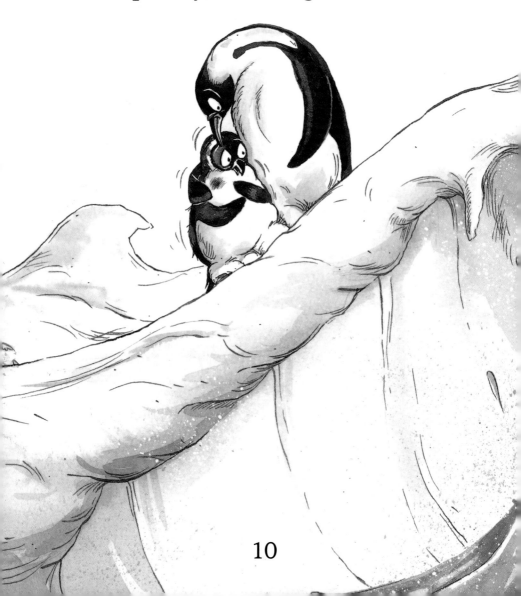

"Just try," said Ma. "I'll get into the water and you can jump to me."

So Pippin said he would try.

He closed
his eyes.

He held his
breath.

He teetered
at the edge.

12

"After three, Pippin," shouted Ma.
"One... two... three... JUMP!"

"I can't, I'm too scared!"

Pippin sat down and wept.

"I'll never be a proper penguin!"

"You are already," said Ma.

"No, I'm not!" cried Pippin. "Proper penguins swim and catch fish. How can I catch fish if I'm too scared to jump in the water?"

"It just takes courage," said Ma.

"What's courage?" asked Pippin.

"Can you hear a voice inside you saying 'You can do it!' and another

voice saying 'No you can't!'?
Courage is when you make the
'can do it' voice louder than the
'can't do it' voice," Ma explained.

"But it isn't easy, is it?" said Pippin.

"Well, I've got an idea!" Ma replied.

"Sometimes courage is easier to find when we help each other. So why don't we all jump in together?"

Pippin liked that idea very much.
So Ma called the other young
penguins to the edge of the iceberg.

They all lined up, side by side.

"After three," shouted Ma.

"One... two... three... JUMP!"

In they jumped! Pippin dipped and dived and splashed and swam.

"Well done!" cheered Ma.

"You've done it, Pippin!"

Pippin was thrilled. He played happily in the water.

24

"Watch me!" he shouted.

"See how deep I can dive!"

25

And all the penguins
watched as Pippin
disappeared below
the waves. Then
they waited for
him to come
back up.

27

Ma was starting to worry. Then,
suddenly, up popped Pippin!
He scrambled on to the iceberg.
"What happened?" asked Ma.

"A fish..." coughed Pippin.
"You caught your first fish on
your first swim? Well done!"
said Ma, proudly.

"No!" said Pippin. "The fish
tried to catch me!"

Hopscotch has been specially designed to fit the requirements of the National Literacy Strategy. It offers real books by top authors and illustrators for children developing their reading skills.

There are 12 Hopscotch stories to choose from:

Marvin, the Blue Pig
0 7496 4473 7 (hbk)
Written by Karen Wallace, illustrated by Lisa Williams
0 7496 4619 5 (pbk)

Plip and Plop
0 7496 4474 5 (hbk)
Written by Penny Dolan, illustrated by Lisa Smith
0 7496 4620 9 (pbk)

The Queen's Dragon
0 7496 4472 9 (hbk)
Written by Anne Cassidy, illustrated by Gwyneth Williamson
0 7496 4618 7 (pbk)

Flora McQuack
0 7496 4475 3 (hbk)
Written by Penny Dolan, illustrated by Kay Widdowson
0 7496 4621 7 (pbk)

Willie the Whale
0 7496 4477 X (hbk)
Written by Joy Oades, illustrated by Barbara Vagnozzi
0 7496 4623 3 (pbk)

Naughty Nancy
0 7496 4476 1 (hbk)
Written by Anne Cassidy, illustrated by Desideria Guicciardini
0 7496 4622 5 (pbk)

Run!
0 7496 4698 5 (hbk)
Written by Sue Ferraby, illustrated by Fabiano Fiorin
0 7496 4705 1 (pbk)

The Playground Snake
0 7496 4699 3 (hbk)
Written by Brian Moses, illustrated by David Mostyn
0 7496 4706 X (pbk)

"Sausages!"
0 7496 4700 0 (hbk)
Written by Anne Adeney, illustrated by Roger Fereday
0 7496 4707 8 (pbk)

The Truth about Hansel and Gretel
0 7496 4701 9 (hbk)
Written by Karina Law, illustrated by Elke Counsell
0 7496 4708 6 (pbk)

Pippin's Big Jump
0 7496 4703 5 (hbk)
Written by Hilary Robinson, illustrated by Sarah Warburton
0 7496 4710 8 (pbk)

Whose Birthday Is It?
0 7496 4702 7 (hbk)
Written by Sherryl Clark, illustrated by Jan Smith
0 7496 4709 4 (pbk)